LONG BEFORE
GOBLINS BUILT AN EMPIRE
ENSLAVING HUMANITY,
HUMANS LIVED IN
HARMONY WITH THE
WORLD & SPIRIT.

WITH THE AID
OF ELVES, ARDILA
JOURNEYS TO RECOVER
THE COSMIC HARP WHICH
CAN RESTORE BALANCE
TO THE WORLD &
ITS INHABITANTS.

Ardila in the Land of Goblin

By

C. K. Niebergall

Dedicated to the Earth with all its Inhabitants

With Deep Gratitude to my Family & Friends...
Thank You for all the Love & Support along the journey.
Without you, This would not exist...

MINE FOR WATER
GO FOR THE GOLD
FRESH DRINKING WATER

Table of Contents

Welcome back Ardila!
We've been expecting you!

We've watched humans grow, create & evolve...
Unseen by normal human eyes,
we've been helping you.
No one is ever really alone...

There was once a time when humans
lived in harmony with the planet.
They cultivated a society based on
love, compassion & forgiveness...
But goblins came & disrupted that
way of life & then it was forgotten...

In this infinite universe, everything changes &
now the goblin's cycle is coming to an end...

But before we get to that
let's journey through time to see
how this all came to be...

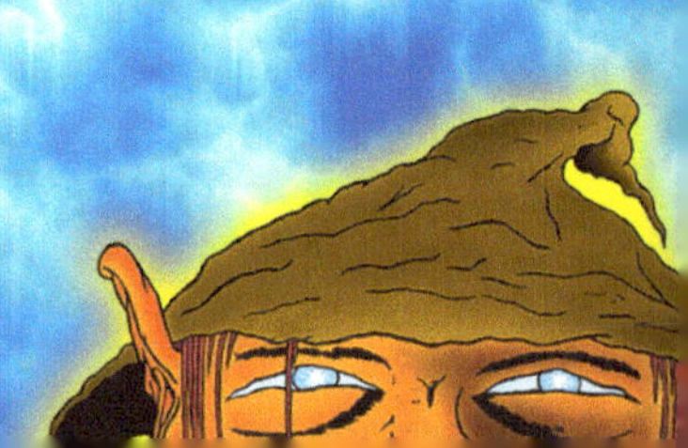

- CHAPTER 1 -
CONCEIVING COSMOS

From the Great Cosmos
of immaculate design,
inner & outer worlds
are woven through
the fabric of time...

Fire kindles Light
Air carries Seed
Water nourishes Life
Earth gives Birth...

Humans grew & evolved, interconnected with their environment.
Plants & animals nourished & guided them. A symbiotic
relationship grew & flourished with fresh creative abundance...

They lived in groups developing skills to manage survival.
Great feasts & celebrations fostered cooperation & community.
The elements were honored in prayer with music & chant.

Humans discovered plants as a key for opening the spirit world. Resulting connections with animal spirits & other mystical entities fostered teachings of compassion, oneness & love, & these were shared amongst the community. Humans recognized & bonded with their spiritual nature. They communicated with intelligences from other dimensions of space & time. And they created a sacred tool, known as the cosmic harp to harmonize heart, mind & soul...

Living from inner peace brought growth & abundance as humans found their place at one with all.

Likewise, connecting with the stars, opened minds to knowledge from afar...

5

Then a new cycle began to emerge. In order to continue evolution, humans would need to face a challenge- the dissonance & chaos of goblins. Humans did what they could to prepare. Schools were built by the wise to teach the experienced mysteries of the universe. Knowledge, maps & musical harmonics were recorded into a visual language that all could understand.

But the goblins came quickly & blocked connections to the spirit world. This had unexpected effects on the community. Abundance shifted to scarcity & people claimed food, knowledge & territory. Ardila, along with the few elders remaining at that time, sought to preserve, teach & protect all sacred teachings of the ancestors.

Scarcity forced people to seek new resources. Strange edibles were added to the human diet which altered perception & behavior. Ragna, one of the wise teachers, was first to experiment...
Hmmm... What is this? Let's harvest some...
So Ragna prepared more of this strange brew & as he sampled he was lured into the goblin realm where he met Virosa, Lord of the goblins.
Hey... This tastes pretty good! But wait... What's happening to me?!
I'm Virosa! You Ragna... are to become a king among humans & rule. You'll have all your desires fulfilled. Just destroy Ardila, then retrieve the book of knowledge for yourself. Ardila is not the controller of knowledge, the decider of who can be taught. It is your right, Ragna. Now be the all powerful leader & harvest our gold!

When Ragna woke up he was feeling confused. However, he remembered what Virosa told him & felt seduced into the plan... He would eliminate the wise elders, rewrite their teachings & crown himself king & ruler over all.

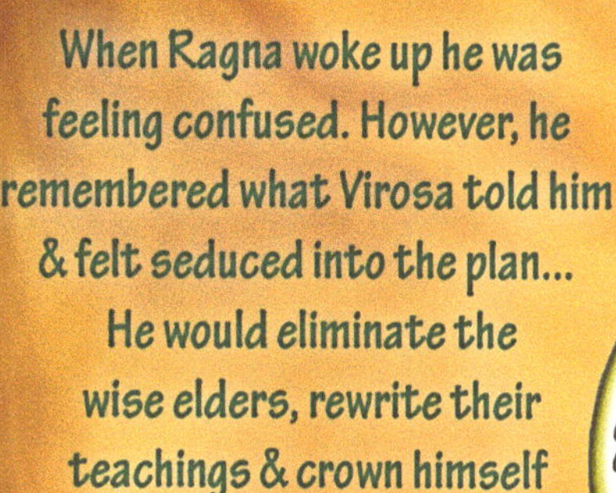

Luring them into the valley, Ragna let loose a dam he had prepared & drowned all the wise teachers... With a final breath, Ardila shouted at him...

With Ardila gone, Ragna took over. He hoarded the ancient's wisdom, distributed rewritten material & strengthened his power as leader. Most people obeyed & followed. They were ignorant of the truth about what happened to the elders.

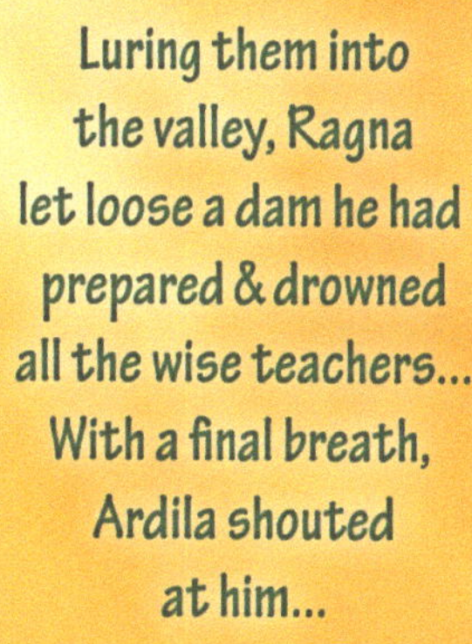

Ragna began to produce more of the substance he drank, which eventually became the sacred drink. Through its widespread use, perception became limited to focus on matter as the only reality. Depression & amnesia became states of being. Humans' spiritual nature was lost. Everyone wandered about, defending territory & claiming ownership of all the elements. People lived in fear, stole, hoarded & made others into enemies.

Artificial laws were created to control this chaos. These human laws destroyed the integrity of natural law then multiplied into endless numbers of extreme laws & restrictions. Sacred plants were outlawed & became taboo. Ranga was empowered with control & authority over how people lived. By the power of these laws, Ragna restricted the free will of people, and often people became jealous of freedom & agreed with the punishment of anyone who found it.

As Ragna gained more & more power, so did Virosa. Under Virosa's control, Ragna created an army of his most trusted followers to serve the law & ensure all humans obeyed.

The goblins' system expanded enormously,
consuming everything. It exploited the
land & resources, & enslaved every
creature to serve the system's needs.
The empire was divided into sections of
those with too much & those with too little.

MINE FOR WATER
WASTE
GO FOR THE GOLD
FINISH
FRESH DRINKING WATER

Below was called Baja where the slaves
lived clustered, working away in the mine. Above was called
Alta where the consumers lived in extravagant abundance.
Time passed, until finally... the system used up all the
resources & began to collapse. Its pinnacle had come...
Ardila was reborn....

- CHAPTER 2 -
A THEATRICAL MOCK-UP
FOR THE NEWCOMERS

Ardila was reborn into the land of goblins. He grew up much like everyone else
in the lower part of Alta. He learned to obey the law. He received medicines
& countless shots from the doctors. He went to the schools where everything
to train the mind was taught: language, numbers, history, science, etc...

One couldn't help but question all this as it all seemed to contradict itself. Under the umbrella of division & confusion, many sensed a strange urge to rebel. Also, something was felt to be missing. In bed at night, the dream state was no longer understood, so few could bring themselves to trust it. Therefore, it was ignored. If you can't touch it, it's not real; it's not been taught. The more system knowledge a person was able to demonstrate, the more authority the person was offered.

You mean, I have to climb that to survive here?!
These humans were taught to believe that they had achieved the greatest advancements of all time, far beyond their "primitive" ancestors. Quality was traded for efficiency & competition replaced cooperation as the way of life. Like so many others, Ardila found this all very confusing.
You must choose an identity. Who do you want to be?
Gotta stay cool kid & stick with the trend... Don't get out of line or you'll be rejected 'til you die...
See, it's all set up for you & me. All we do is work & choose a stereotype to be...
16

Ardila's life coach had some suggestions. "Why don't you start at Mr. Fartherway's office. He needs people & is highly famed. As his servant, eventually you'll gain reputation & get paid more. Also, if you're good, you might gain your own servants. I'll sign you up."

So Ardila worked at the man's office helping with chores & errands. Once a week all the servants groomed Mr. Fartherway's body. As time passed, Ardila began to notice that even though he was a pawn at the office he had slowly gained status in society. His boss was owner of many operations including the mine, residential lots, schools & media. In fact, since he was so loyal to his boss, it didn't take long before Ardila began to have servants. He was rewarded with job advancement & admiration.

However, everything changed one day when Ardila walked into the media room at the office. There he saw all the programs being written & realized that social behavior was a direct result of what was being fed into people's minds. At first he thought it was good for the economy, but changed his mind when he recognized how these negative images were implanted into everyone's mindset. Brains stagnated, & became disconnected entirely from their true nature. People were then predictable, divided & zombified...

After this discovery, Ardila became more curious.
He began to really explore the area where he lived.
He encountered a fence dividing the land.
There he saw two fellows in ragged
clothes, reaching underneath the fence.
"Please sir, we're starving down here,
could you spare a buck?" one asked.
Suddenly out of nowhere, an officer appeared
& began beating the men to force them away.
"Run away boy! These guys are dangerous,"
the officer warned. Frightened, Ardila bolted
& returned home. Later that night he saw
a story on the news reporting this incident...

On his way down, Ardila came to the fence again & wriggled his way under. Not far on the other side he ran into a crowd. A person named Solis spoke to Ardila in a gruff tone. "What'cha doing here boy? You don't belong here." "I'm trying to understand the lies I heard on the news," Ardila explained. "So I came to see for myself what's really going on." Ardila told the story about the 2 guys, the officer, & how it was reported. "Well, then hang out with us & see," said Solis, "I'll take you around & show you what's happening. Everyone works in the mine & tries to feed their families... There used to be a school but people needed to work more than anything, so they didn't go & the school shut down. Food is scarce here & water is expensive. Tell us about where you're from." Ardila didn't know what to say. He remembered the abundance of food & water, the products filling stores & all the comforts, more than anyone needed. He stood silent.

MINE FOR WATER

WASTE

"Come. Let's go collect some water," said Solis. In the water line, people were pushing & fighting their way through... When they finally got to the gate, the taxman gave them a hard time...

FRESH DRINKING WATER

1 COIN

"Come to our home," said Solis, "My family would like to meet you." Upon arriving, Ardila couldn't have imagined a warmer welcome. The family offered him food & bedding although the house was just one room. "Solis, have you taken him to the tree yet?" asked the man's wife. "No, maybe tomorrow." "The tree?" responded Ardila. "It's called the tree of control. Yeah, you should see it if you really want to know what's going on. We can go tomorrow if you want," said Solis. "Sounds great!" Ardila responded. The next morning, along the way, they met a friend of Solis who was selling handmade beads.
"Hey Solis, How are you brother?" said Iah.
"Iah! Good to see you, man. This is Ardila. I'm taking him to the tree. He's from Alta, checking it out here," responded Solis.
"No way man, from Alta? hmmm... I'll come along & tell stories to the kid," said Iah.

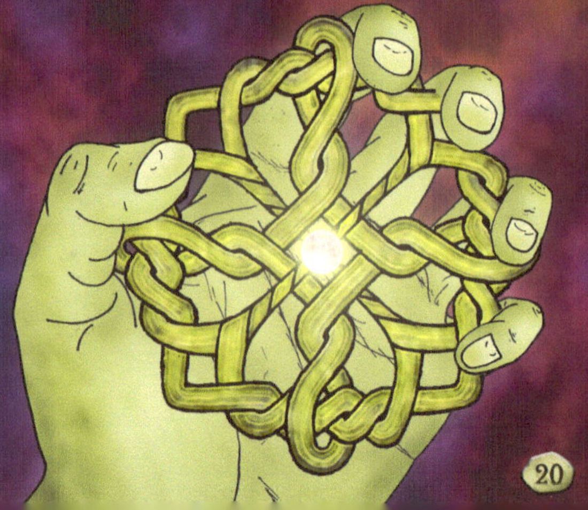

Before they arrived at the tree the 3 stopped to talk. The men warned Ardila about the dangers of the tree, & they shared a ceremonial pipe. "Here Ardila, have this, it's an amulet I've made for prayers. May it protect you," said Iah "Thank you, Iah!" responded Ardila, & they continued toward the tree...

"Here it is! This is the tree of control," said Solis.
"It keeps the system in control by squeezing the life out of those living in Baja, while stimulating those in Alta to consume more. Where this is all leading & why, no one seems to know. But this is what's going on in our world."
"This is insane! In Alta we have fountains flourishing with clean water being wasted. Why is this happening?" shouted Ardila. "Best you get back home Ardila before it gets any later & you're stuck here... with us," said Solis.

So Ardila left his thanks & made his way up the hill back home. He climbed & climbed until he was exhausted. As he hiked, thoughts & emotions bombarded his mind with endless questions. He sat on a log to contemplate...
Fragments of his life flashed before his eyes, as he remembered & connected dots of what he'd seen...
One side has way too much, the other way too little. Who's controlling this? Why?
Ardila's head was spinning & his thoughts were stalled. He got up & began to stomp on the log in frustration. And Whoooooosh!..... He slipped, knocking himself out.
BAM
What's going on? Why must I leave? & go where?
A canoe? What goblins? They'll do what?
Instantaneously, he dissolved into a web of energy which interconnected all entities in a myriad of infinite realities.

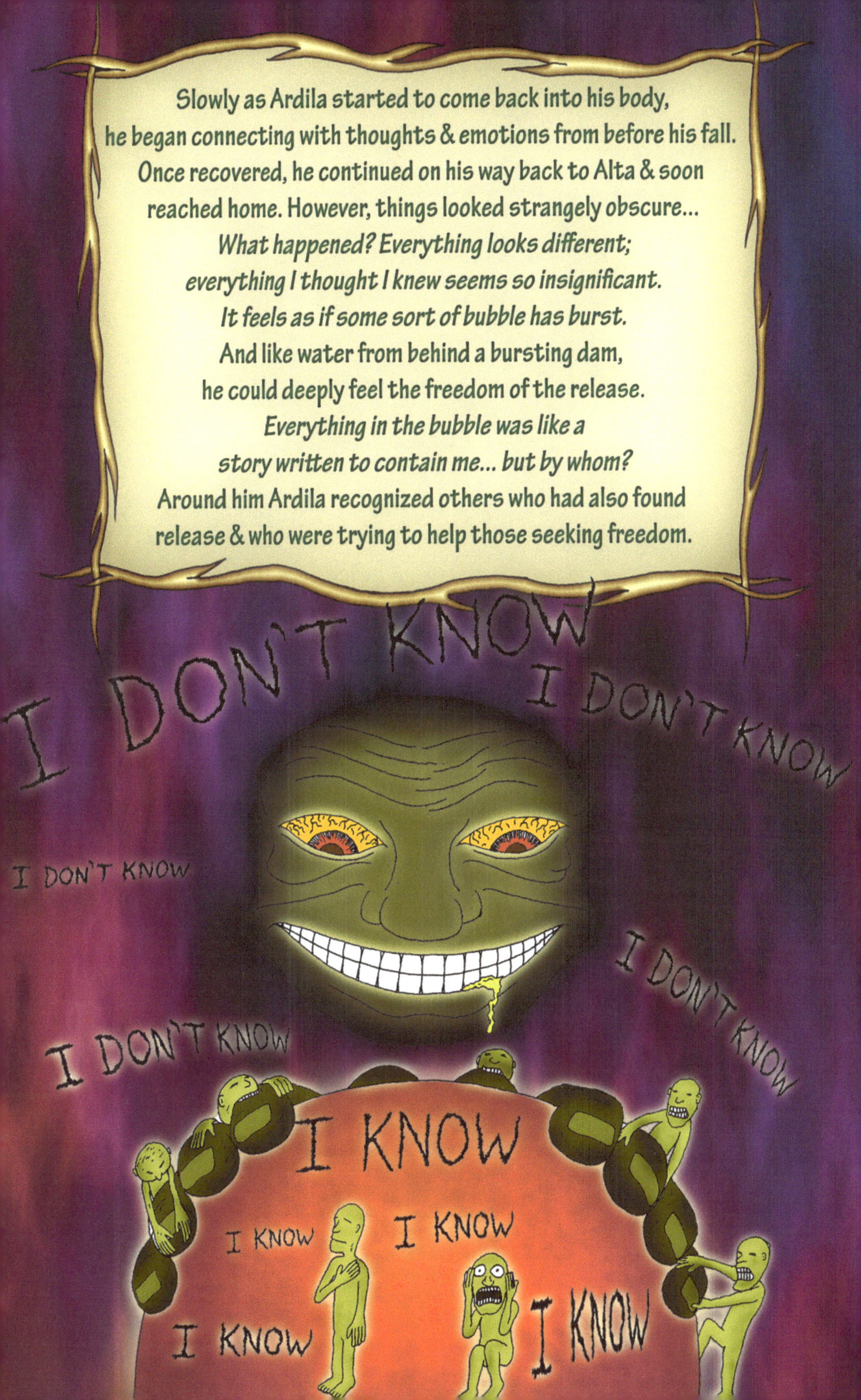

Slowly as Ardila started to come back into his body,
he began connecting with thoughts & emotions from before his fall.
Once recovered, he continued on his way back to Alta & soon
reached home. However, things looked strangely obscure...
What happened? Everything looks different;
everything I thought I knew seems so insignificant.
It feels as if some sort of bubble has burst.
And like water from behind a bursting dam,
he could deeply feel the freedom of the release.
Everything in the bubble was like a
story written to contain me... but by whom?
Around him Ardila recognized others who had also found
release & who were trying to help those seeking freedom.
I DON'T KNOW
I DON'T KNOW
I DON'T KNOW
I DON'T KNOW
I DON'T KNOW
I KNOW
I KNOW
I KNOW
I KNOW
I KNOW

Ardila decided to help as well, but met mostly resistance. He talked amongst the contained people. Some were shy, & others were interactive, but many resisted release & some even got angry. But, the released ones continued to try & help those still trapped within bubbles.
Why would that matter? Those in power understand me. I identify with their messages.
Excuse me, Lady. Have you ever questioned our leaders? or have you wondered why we can't find a minute to stop, observe & think for ourselves?
Of course you do! They have studied you; they know what you feel; they have used scientists, psychologists & spies to analyze you.
They offer you anything from trash to honey to keep you in line & line their pockets with money...
So much stimulation... overwhelming materialism. It's insanity!
24

After awhile, Ardila grew tired of this struggle & left. He remembered the amulet Iah had given him & enclosed it in his hand. Immediately he heard a voice in his head saying, "Go Ardila... Go Now!" Ardila was confused. Soon though, he saw a goblin leap out at him. He turned & ran as fast as he could. The goblin chased right behind him.

Ah, the canoe! My way out...
Ardila followed alongside the river & came across a canoe. He pushed it into the water & sailed away. He passed tempting gold piles & paddled through an unknown cave.
END OF THE WORLD
FFFRREEEEEEEEE

"Ah, free at last!" Ardila exclaimed, as he guided his canoe to the bank of the river. He stood in awe, as he gazed around the beautiful garden which bloomed perpetually with abundant life. A voice called down from the bridge, "Come on in, Ardila, you're welcome here. This is the Crystal Shrine, an eternal place, which can never be destroyed. The Land of Goblin, where you came from is falling away... It's now time for the Great Awakening... Come, there is much to do... By the way, I am Kunzei." Ardila was led to a waterfall where he was invited to bathe & swim in the pond on his own. He experienced his thoughts washing away & his emotions stabilizing as if everything he was thinking & feeling was completely irrelevant to the moment.

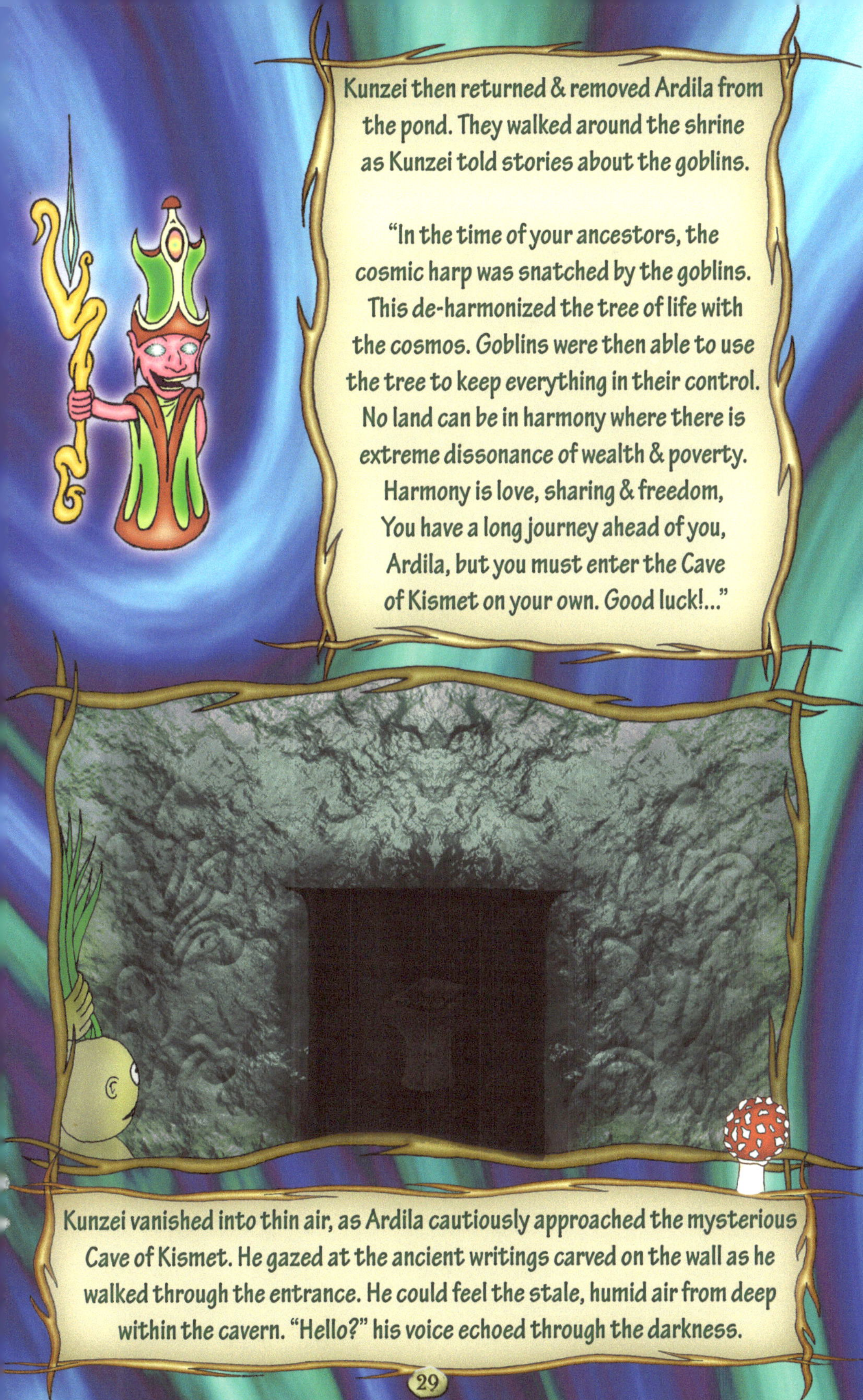

Kunzei then returned & removed Ardila from the pond. They walked around the shrine as Kunzei told stories about the goblins.

"In the time of your ancestors, the cosmic harp was snatched by the goblins. This de-harmonized the tree of life with the cosmos. Goblins were then able to use the tree to keep everything in their control. No land can be in harmony where there is extreme dissonance of wealth & poverty. Harmony is love, sharing & freedom, You have a long journey ahead of you, Ardila, but you must enter the Cave of Kismet on your own. Good luck!..."

Kunzei vanished into thin air, as Ardila cautiously approached the mysterious Cave of Kismet. He gazed at the ancient writings carved on the wall as he walked through the entrance. He could feel the stale, humid air from deep within the cavern. "Hello?" his voice echoed through the darkness.

Suddenly, Ardila began to feel his pouch burning hot... He reached in to find the amulet glowing vigorously... Like a magnet, its power pulled him toward a pedestal holding a book. "Wow, this is amazing! This book has the amulet carved into it," Ardila said as he wiped off a thick layer of dust off the book's cover.

Unable to resist, he opened the book & felt a rush of energy enveloping his being. As if placed in a room filled with mirrors, he felt an infinite sequence of macrocosmic & microcosmic realities. Merging back into his body in the cave, he noticed the room filling with smoke. Out of its midst emerged a bizarre looking creature. Ardila stood stunned as it spoke...

Welcome back, Ardila!
So great to see you again!
I am Nusku & you're in a state of amnesia.

Not to worry, deep down you already know everything.
It will all come back to you shortly. Remember your fall?
When you returned, you realized you had changed.
Where do you think you went?

When one journeys & discovers something of immeasurable value,
it is gracious to leave guidelines or a map for future travelers.
It also is helpful in finding your own way back.

Don't forget your journey through the Land of Goblin,
where you experienced the areas of growth one
must go through for spiritual development...

There will be guides & misguides. Pay attention!!
And always remind yourself of your quest...
try not to lose yourself in amazement...

Some creatures see in black & white only...
Imagine explaining color to them...
How would you describe yellow?... green?
Could they even accept the fact of its existence?
What would that imply?

When you stop chewing on thoughts,
What do you see? Open your mouth & listen.

Reflect on how your intention
defines your destination,
then... drink this...

Smoke filled the room again & Nusku disappeared...
Ardila meditated for days without food, until
he felt ready. Then he drank the magic potion...

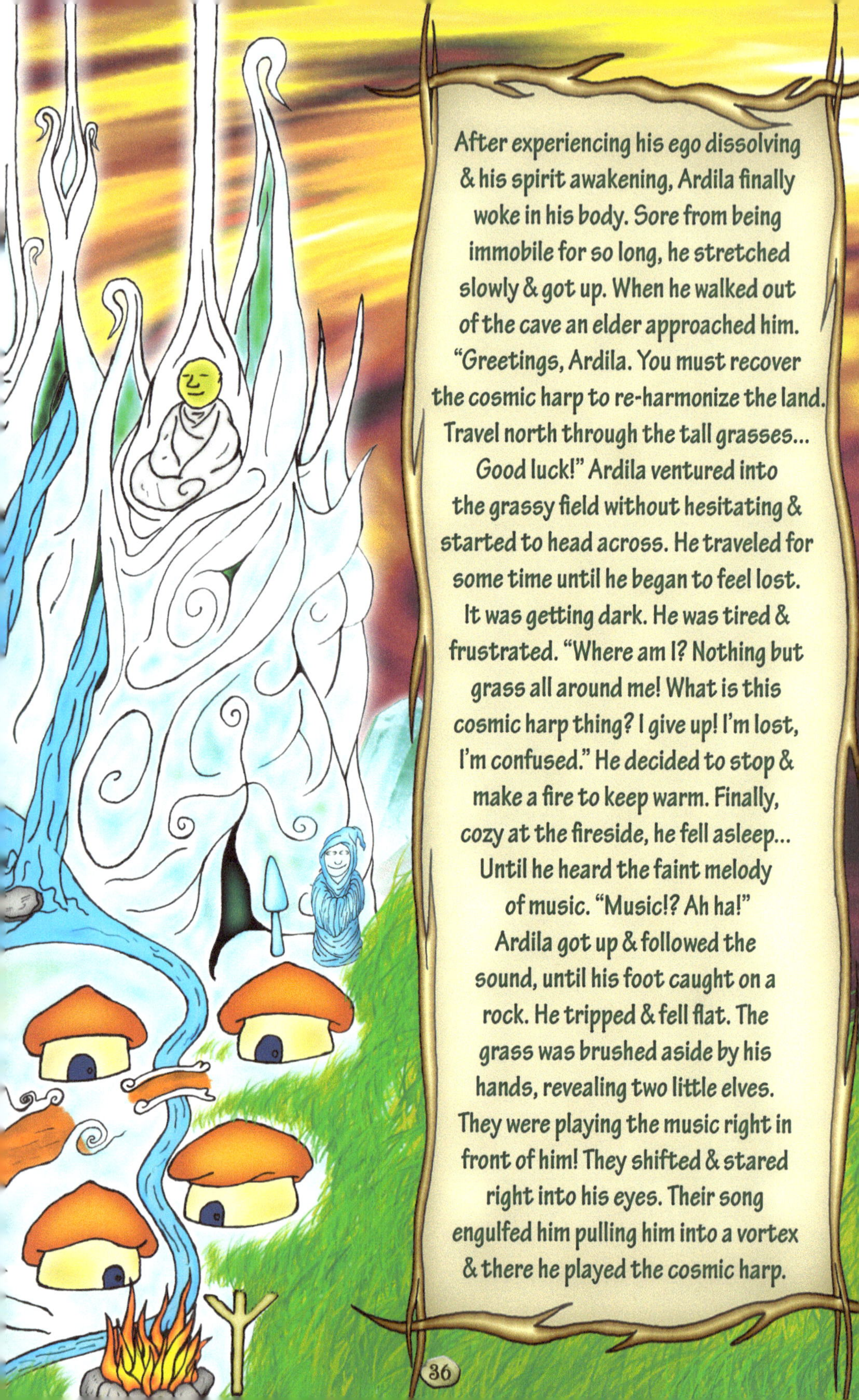

After experiencing his ego dissolving & his spirit awakening, Ardila finally woke in his body. Sore from being immobile for so long, he stretched slowly & got up. When he walked out of the cave an elder approached him. "Greetings, Ardila. You must recover the cosmic harp to re-harmonize the land. Travel north through the tall grasses... Good luck!" Ardila ventured into the grassy field without hesitating & started to head across. He traveled for some time until he began to feel lost. It was getting dark. He was tired & frustrated. "Where am I? Nothing but grass all around me! What is this cosmic harp thing? I give up! I'm lost, I'm confused." He decided to stop & make a fire to keep warm. Finally, cozy at the fireside, he fell asleep... Until he heard the faint melody of music. "Music!? Ah ha!" Ardila got up & followed the sound, until his foot caught on a rock. He tripped & fell flat. The grass was brushed aside by his hands, revealing two little elves. They were playing the music right in front of him! They shifted & stared right into his eyes. Their song engulfed him pulling him into a vortex & there he played the cosmic harp.

He felt himself opening up into the highest spirit world...
His body & surroundings became smaller & smaller as he
spiraled out & melted into one with the universe. Overwhelming
feelings of cosmic ecstasy soaked his soul into union with eternity.

Luminescent strands of energy wove Ardila back into existence & released him. Ardila found himself inside an energy vehicle of 2 interlocking triangles, hovering face to face with the flower's orb. In a graceful sweep, Ardila landed & was greeted by an elder. "Ardila! Quickly, you must get back to the Land of Goblin, I'll take you as close as I can," said Enti as he wove a cyclone with his wand that engulfed them. They vanished & reappeared before a forest. "Ok, Ardila, this is the path to enter the Land of Goblin. We'll see each other very soon." Enti spoke & disappeared. With the harp on his back, Ardila entered the forest.

As he got closer he could feel the atmosphere getting denser & darker.
"I can barely see. How am I going to find my way back?" he said aloud.
"I can help you. Come, follow my lantern," said a goblin who appeared mysteriously.
40

Ardila accepted as he saw no other option.
They continued down the path when suddenly an arm
reached out & pulled him back. "You must come with me,
you're not ready yet," spoke a voice out of the darkness.
Ardila felt himself being dragged out of the goblin's sight.
41

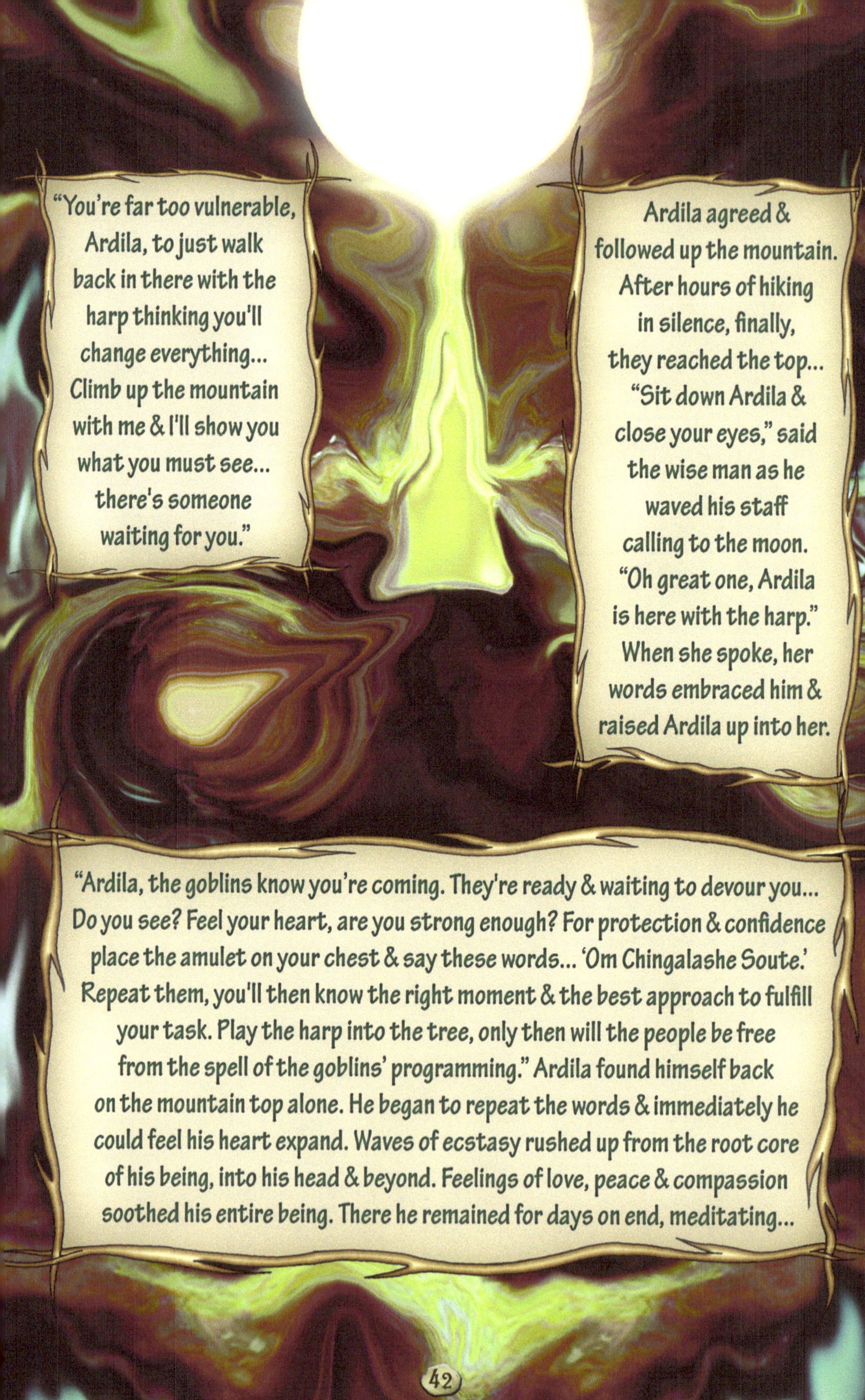

"You're far too vulnerable, Ardila, to just walk back in there with the harp thinking you'll change everything... Climb up the mountain with me & I'll show you what you must see... there's someone waiting for you."

Ardila agreed & followed up the mountain. After hours of hiking in silence, finally, they reached the top... "Sit down Ardila & close your eyes," said the wise man as he waved his staff calling to the moon. "Oh great one, Ardila is here with the harp." When she spoke, her words embraced him & raised Ardila up into her.

"Ardila, the goblins know you're coming. They're ready & waiting to devour you... Do you see? Feel your heart, are you strong enough? For protection & confidence place the amulet on your chest & say these words... 'Om Chingalashe Soute.' Repeat them, you'll then know the right moment & the best approach to fulfill your task. Play the harp into the tree, only then will the people be free from the spell of the goblins' programming." Ardila found himself back on the mountain top alone. He began to repeat the words & immediately he could feel his heart expand. Waves of ecstasy rushed up from the root core of his being, into his head & beyond. Feelings of love, peace & compassion soothed his entire being. There he remained for days on end, meditating...

One day, he heard an inner voice say "Ardila, you are ready. You must go now. Remember all you've learned & experienced, but most importantly, follow your heart." So Ardila made his way back down the mountain & followed the path into the Land of Goblin. He approached from the hillside to have a clear view. He could see the goblins waiting at the entrance. Quietly, he slipped into the water & swam his way up into the land until he was far enough to see the stream's headwaters.

Then, cautiously he got out. No-one was in sight... He hiked up the hill towards the tree- when out of nowhere an old friend saw him. "Ardila! Where've you been buddy? We've all been looking for you. You've been missed." "Ah, got no time Lin, I must keep going," Ardila replied.

Then he heard a different voice... "Arghhh... Ardila! Where do you think you're going?!" screeched a goblin from behind Lin. Ardila began to run as fast as he could for the tree... He was almost there when Virosa leaped in front of him...
Well, well, Ardila... Come here... I've got a special reserve just for you! Take the Gold or meet the goblin army & prepare to Die!
"I'll never give in to you goblins!" Ardila shouted. Hundreds of goblins surrounded him. Frozen stiff & unsure of what to do, he remembered the words 'Om Chingalashe Soute'. As he spoke them, he could feel a light radiate in his heart. He could see the great lotus beam with life.

The physical world of matter began to merge with the spirit world as Nusku appeared hurling a flame to create an auric shield around Ardila.
Ardila played the harp, feeling the channeling of ancestors flow through his being. "Ahgghaaa," shrieked the goblins as they panicked.
More elfin elders seemed to appear out of thin air.
Curiously, people approached to see what was happening. Ardila passed the harp around...
& everyone played, awakening & connecting themselves to their spiritual nature. Transcending dimensional space, the lower realm of war & dissonance was left behind.

Humans awoke from division & confusion joining together in harmonic recognition. Alta & Baja merged together as the tree of control was freed & became the tree of life once again. The goblins contracted themselves & vanished into oblivion. Humankind gathered with ancestors in unison, transcending themselves, becoming one with the universe. The returning flow of peace & bliss felt ever so sweet.

MINE FOR WATER
GO FOR THE GOLD
FRESH DRINKING WATER
WASTE

Did you think that was the end?
Ha... it's merely the beginning...